W9-DDZ-461

Dance, Mice, Dance!

หนูเต้นระบำ!

English / Thai

Dance, Mice, Dance!

หนูเต้นระบำ!

English/Thai

Retold by Kuang-ts'ai Hao; Illustrated by Stefano Tartarotti
Thai translation by Prachumporn Laohajinda

This bilingual edition is co-published & distributed
by
Pan Asian Publications (USA) Inc.
29564 Union City Blvd., Union City, California 94587 USA
Tel: (510) 475-1185 Fax: (510) 475-1489

ISBN 1-57227-004-7

Printed in Hong Kong

Dance, Mice, Dance!

หนูเต้นระบำ!

English / Thai

Retold by Kuang-ts'ai Hao; Illustrated by Stefano Tartarotti
Thai translation by Prachumporn Laohajinda

Grimm Press

Once upon a time there was a man named Jimmy Tune. No one knew him by that name, but if you said "Jimmy the Magic Flute," everyone knew who he was.

When Jimmy played a happy melody, sad people smiled. When he played a gentle melody, naughty children behaved.

Each time Jimmy performed, the audience cheered and clapped wildly, "Encore! Encore!"

กาลครั้งหนึ่งนานมาแล้ว มีชายคนหนึ่งชื่อจิมมี่ ทูน ไม่มีใครรู้จักชื่อจริงของเขา แต่ทุกคนรู้จักเขาในนาม "จิมมี่กับขลุ่ยวิเศษ"

เมื่อใดที่จิมมี่เป่าเพลงอันแสนสุข คนที่มีความทุกข์จะยิ้ม เมื่อใดที่เขาเป่าเพลงอันอ่อนโยน เด็กที่ซุกซนจะทำตัวดี

ทุกครั้งที่จิมมี่เป่าขลุ่ย ผู้ชมจะปรบมือให้กำลังใจอย่างท้วมท้น "ขออีกเพลง! ขออีกเพลง!"

As Jimmy's success made him prouder and prouder, he practiced less and less.

Alcohol became his only friend, and each day he drank until he was dizzy. He played so poorly that he was no longer called "Jimmy the Magic Flute." Now people called him "Jimmy Out of Tune."

Finally, he lost his job.

ความสำเร็จทำให้จิมมี่ลืมตัว และฝึกเป่าขลุ่ยน้อยลงทุกวัน

เหล้าเท่านั้นที่เป็นเพื่อนเขา และดื่มเหล้าทุกวันจนมึนศีรษะ จิมมี่เป่าขลุ่ยเลวลง จนไม่มีใครเรียกเขาว่า "จิมมี่กับขลุ่ยวิเศษ" แต่ถูกเรียกว่า "จิมมี่ผู้ไม่มีเพลง"

ในที่สุดเขาตกงาน

After that, Jimmy pretended he was blind. He played his flute and begged for money to get by.

Even though he looked pitiful, he didn't collect very much money. Often he ate only one meal in two or three days.

หลังจากนั้น จิมมี่แสร้งทำเป็นคนตาบอด เขาเป่าขลุ่ยและขอทานเป็นเครื่องยังชีพ

แม้เขาจะดูน่าสงสาร แต่เขาไม่สามารถขอเงินได้มากนัก บ่อยครั้งที่เขากินอาหารเพียงมื้อเดียวในเวลาสองถึงสามวัน

One unlucky day, Jimmy went into an alley to find something to eat.

Some impish little boys arrived just as he was rummaging through the garbage. They shouted, "Quick, come and see! The blind man can really see!"

The little devils surrounded Jimmy, laughing and making fun of him. They stepped on his glasses and crushed them to bits.

วันที่โชคร้าย จิมมี่เดินเข้าตรอกเพื่อค้นหาเศษอาหาร
ขณะที่เขากำลังคุ้ยกองขยะ เด็กเกเรกลุ่มหนึ่งเดินผ่านมา
และตะโกนว่า "มานี่สิ! คนตาบอดมองเห็นได้"
เด็กเกเรกลุ่มนั้นล้อมตัวจิมมี่ หัวเราะเยาะราวกับเขาเป็นตัวตลก
ยิ่งกว่านั้นเหยียบแว่นตาเขาจนแตกกระจาย

A group of mice stood watching nearby. When they saw Jimmy being bullied for no reason at all, they took out a flashlight and made the terrifying shadow of a monster on the wall. The little boys cried out in fright and quickly took flight.

หนูกลุ่มหนึ่งมองเหตุการณ์อยู่ใกล้เคียง เมื่อเห็นจิมมี่ถูกเกเรโดยไม่มีเหตุผล หนูแกว่งไฟฉาย ทำให้เกิดเงาน่ากลัวเหมือนสัตว์ประหลาดบนกำแพง เด็กเกเรกลุ่มนั้นตะโกนร้องและวิ่งหนีด้วยความตกใจ

Jimmy and the mice became very good friends.

When Jimmy was hungry, the mice stole food for him. When Jimmy finished eating, he played happy music and the mice danced joyfully.

"Dance, mice, dance!" The lively notes from Jimmy's flute danced into the hearts of the mice.

จิมมี่และหนูกลายเป็นเพื่อนรักกัน

เมื่อจิมมี่หิว หนูจะขโมยอาหารมาให้ เมื่อเขากินอิ่มจะเป่าเพลงให้หนูเต้นระบำอย่างสนุกสนาน

"เต้นระบำ, หนู, เต้นระบำ!" โน๊ตเพลงอันมีชีวิตชีวาของจิมมี่ซึมซาบเข้าหัวใจของหนูตัวน้อยๆ

One day, the owner of a fancy restaurant passed by. The owner thought that Jimmy could perform magic, because the sound of his flute made the mice dance. The owner's eyes brightened. He was sure he had found a great new act for his restaurant!

Jimmy was thrilled that someone wanted him to perform on stage again. "Dance, mice, dance! We are going to give a splendid performance!"

วันหนึ่งเจ้าของร้านอาหารผ่านมา เขาคิดว่าการแสดงของจิมมี่วิเศษมาก เพราะเสียงขลุ่ยทำให้หนูเต้นระบำได้ ตาเขาลุกวาวเมื่อแน่ใจว่าได้ค้นพบการแสดงอันยิ่งใหญ่สำหรับร้านอาหารเขา!

จิมมี่ตื่นเต้นเมื่อรู้ว่ามีผู้ต้องการให้เขาแสดงบนเวทีอีกครั้ง "เต้นระบำ, หนู, เต้นระบำ! เราจะเสนอการแสดงที่วิเศษสุด!"

Ballet, tap, waltz, folk, the hula-hula... Old, new, fast, or slow, there was not one dance the mice didn't know.

"Dance, mice, dance!" The restaurant was booked every night, and Jimmy became a star again.

แบเล, แท็พ, วอลซ, โพค, ฮูลา-ฮูลา...เก่า, ใหม่, เร็ว หรือ ช้า ไม่มีจังหวะใด ที่หนูเต้นไม่ได้

"เต้นระบำ, หนู, เต้นระบำ!" ร้านอาหารเต็มทุกวัน และจิมมี่กลายเป็นดาราอีกครั้งหนึ่ง

Jimmy no longer worried about money. Now he only worried about how to enjoy himself. Alcohol became his best friend again.

"Dance, mice, dance! Give us new dance steps!" Jimmy treated the mice like machines and never let them rest.

The mice did not eat or sleep well. They had no energy left for dancing and could not keep up with the music.

จิมมี่เลิกวิตกเรื่องเงิน คิดถึงแต่ความสนุกของตน เหล้ากลายเป็นเพื่อนสนิทของเขาอีกครั้ง

"เต้นระบำ, หนู, เต้นระบำ! เจ้าต้องเต้นจังหวะใหม่" จิมมี่ปฏิบัติต่อหนูราวกับหนูเป็นเครื่องจักร ไม่ให้หนูพักผ่อน

หนูกินไม่อิ่ม นอนไม่หลับ ไม่มีกำลังเต้นระบำให้เข้ากับจังหวะเพลง

Business was terrible. The owner warned Jimmy, "Clean up your act, or you'll get sacked!"

The mice told Jimmy that they didn't want dancing to become work. They just wanted to be carefree.

But Jimmy refused to listen. He yelled and cursed. Then he locked the mice away and gave them no food all day.

ธุรกิจตกต่ำ เจ้าของร้านอาหารเตือนจิมมี่
"เจ้าต้องปรับปรุงการแสดง ไม่เช่นนั้นจะถูกไล่ออก!"

หนูบอกจิมมี่ว่าพวกตนต้องการเต้นระบำเพื่อความสนุก ไม่ใช่เพื่องาน
จิมมี่ไม่ยอมฟัง เขาตวาดและด่าหนู ก่อนที่จะขังหนูให้อดอาหารตลอดวัน

The lights came up, the curtains parted, the show started!
"Dance, mice, dance!" But the mice were too hungry and tired. They smelled the delicious food on the tables, and their mouths began to water...

ไฟบนเวทีปรากฏ ม่านเปิด การแสดงเริ่มต้นแล้ว!
"เต้นระบำ, หนู, เต้นระบำ!" พวกหนูต่างหิวโซและเหนื่อย เมื่อได้กลิ่นอาหารอันโอชาบนโต๊ะ หนูน้ำลายไหล...

Finally, the mice could stand it no longer.

They rushed from the stage, snatched a cake and grabbed a steak...

What a disaster! What confusion!

ในที่สุดหนูอดใจไม่ไหว
กระโดดลงจากเวที ฉวยเค้กและคว้าเนื้อชิ้นใหญ่...
ช่างเป็นความหายนะ! สับสนอลหม่าน!

The chaos finally ended. The guests ran away and the mice disappeared.

"Get out of here right now, I say, or I'll have the police take you away!" The owner threw Jimmy out into the street. He walked along, hanging his head. Suddenly, he heard a cat yowling. "Oh, no!" he cried, and ran toward the howling.

เมื่อความวุ่นวายจบลง แขกวิ่งหนี พวกหนูต่างหายตัวไปหมด

"ออกไปจากที่นี่เดี๋ยวนี้ ไม่เช่นนั้นฉันจะให้ตำรวจลากตัวแกออกไป!" เจ้าของร้านอาหารไล่จิมมี่ออกจากร้าน เขาเดินคอตกไปตามถนน ทันใดนั้นได้ยินเสียงคำรามของแมว "โอ้, อย่า!" จิมมี่ร้องและวิ่งไปตามเสียงนั้น

The frightened mice were trapped by a cat. The cat looked at them savagely to see which one was the biggest and fattest to stuff in his mouth.

Suddenly, out leapt Jimmy, waving his flute and shouting. He chased the cat away. The mice were saved!

พวกหนูกลัวจนตัวสั่นเมื่อตกอยู่ในกรงเล็บของแมว แมวจ้องหนูอย่างดุร้าย สายตาสอดส่องมองหาหนูตัวที่อ้วนที่สุดเพื่อเป็นอาหารปาก

ทันใดนั้น จิมมี่กระโดดเข้ามาช่วย มือแกว่งขลุ่ยไล่แมวจนหนีเตลิดไป หนูจึงปลอดภัย

From then on, no one in the city ever heard the name "Jimmy the Magic Flute". But in the countryside, everyone knew the joyful sound of his playing.

"He's here! He's here! That happy man and his happy mice have come to dance and bring us cheer!"

ตั้งแต่นั้นมา ไม่มีใครในเมืองได้ยินชื่อ "จิมมี่กับขลุ่ยวิเศษ"
คนในชนบทเท่านั้นที่รู้จักเสียงขลุ่ยอันร่าเริงของเขา

"เขามาแล้ว! เขามาแล้ว! ชายกับหนูผู้มีความสุข
เต้นระบำเพื่อนำความสนุกสนานมาให้ทุกคน!"

About the Author and the Illustrator

Hao, Kuang-ts'ai (Author)

Hao Kuang-ts'ai is a rare talent in Chinese children's literature. In addition to editing, writing, and illustrating, he is also skilled in layout and design. With his talented artistry, strong intellect and childlike playfulness, he has produced a series of superb books.

Hao understands children. His stories are fluid and relaxing when read aloud and can be easily recited by children who enjoy the aesthetics of language and sound.

Hao Kuang-ts'ai was born in 1961 in Taipei, Taiwan. He graduated from the Law School at National Chengchi University before becoming an author of children's books. His book Wake Up, Emperor! won a top prize for children's literature and his other works also enjoy high acclaim.

Tartarotti, Stefano (Illustrator)

Stefano Tartarotti is a talented new European illustrator. Born in 1968 in Bolzano, Italy, he studied drawing in Milan. As a student, he did illustrations for newspapers and magazines in Rome and Milan. His talent was quickly discovered by local publishers, and his work was selected for display at the "International Exhibition of Children's Book Illustrations in Bologna."

Tartarotti likes to use the language of drawing, which children grasp easily, to tell stories. Rather than drawing things strictly as they appear, he uses fluid, lively strokes to change appearances and convey profound emotions. In Dance, Mice, Dance! the characters' actions and expressions are not exaggerated, but the buildings and trees that form the background to the action are distorted and striking. Characters and scenery therefore, achieve a certain harmony. Tartarotti's technical skill combines with his emotional sensitivity to touch his audience deeply.